INSIDE
THE MIND OF
MARYANN

DARLENE MAKINS

authorHOUSE®

AuthorHouse™
1663 Liberty Drive
Bloomington, IN 47403
www.authorhouse.com
Phone: 1 (800) 839-8640

Published by AuthorHouse 08/10/2017

ISBN: 978-1-5462-0400-8 (sc)
ISBN: 978-1-5462-0399-5 (e)

Maryann was an eleven year old girl that had a lot of friends in the neighborhood. Her parents were split up and she was living with her mother, two brothers, and two sisters. Her mother was working at a grocery store as a cashier and they were on a fixed income; they lived in a run-down apartment building that sometimes didn't have lights in the hallway and was full of mice. The hallway was always filled with big cats and they would be afraid to go in the building because it would be too dark. They lived in the ghetto part of Baltimore and the neighborhood was full of violence because people would be selling drugs, shooting and breaking into people houses all the time. The neighborhood was filled with drunks and drug addicts on every corner; there was trash everywhere and people fighting all the time. Maryann hated where she lived but that area was all her mother could afford to be in. They were poor and had no means of other assistance to help the family. Sometimes they couldn't eat because there were no groceries in the house and her mother refused to get on welfare. Although, they were poor, they were well taken care of and healthy. Her mother did all that she could to provide for her family with the help sometimes from her father.

Every day that she came home from school, she did her homework and then would go outside to play with her friends but for some reason she would always fight in school and fight with her friends but they still kept her as their friend anyway. Maryann was very active in the neighborhood, she knew everyone and would constantly stay after school to hang out in the recreation room painting and working with arts and crafts. On the days that she didn't stay after school, she would hang out with her friends for a little while and then proceed to go home. Once she got home, she would argue with her sisters and brothers about whose turn it was to clean the kitchen. Maryann was a very smart young girl and loved to go to school; she also loved her family and friends but she was very naïve. She started developing early and started doing things out of the ordinary that she would ask herself why she was doing bad things but she never could figure out why she was acting out. She loved to read all the encyclopedias that her mother kept on the bookshelf; her favorite story to read was John Henry.

Maryann's mother was always working late in order for her to make extra money to pay her bills, that she barely had time for her children because most of the time they would be asleep when she got home. Her dad would visit her and her siblings a couple times a week and would have treats for them hidden in the hallway. She always wanted her parents to get back together because she loved both of them so much. Most weekends she spent over her father's house and always felt his love for her. When it was time for her to return home, she never wanted to go home because she had a secret she wanted to tell her father but she never got the chance to tell him because she was afraid and felt he wouldn't believe her. She was dealing with a lot of emotions that she could not understand or why this was happening to her.

One weekend that she stayed with her father, she told him she wanted to come live with him but he told her that she couldn't because no one would be there to care for her while he worked; she got upset but accepted what he told her. When it was time for her to go home, she would cry but leave anyway. Once she arrived home, she went into her room and got into her bed and cried herself to sleep. While she was asleep, her older brother Talbert eased into her room and crawled in the bed with her and started feeling all over her; he then raped her. She begged and pleaded with him to stop but he wouldn't stop. She was fighting and biting him but he kept holding her down. He covered her mouth and told her that if she told anyone he would kill her. When he was finished, he walked towards the door and turned around and whispered to her, not a word or I will kill you. All Maryann could do was lay there and cry herself to sleep.

The very next morning she woke up and got herself ready for school; she walked into the kitchen and there was her mother standing there cooking breakfast.

"Maryann would you like some breakfast? Her mother asked."

In a sad tone Maryann said no.

Her mother asked her if she was alright and she said no.

Maryann sat down at the breakfast table and told her mother that she had something to tell her. But as she started to tell her mother, her brother walked in the kitchen and gave her a mean look and put his hands to his neck as if he was going to choke himself to remind her of what he would do to her. She hurried out of the kitchen and went to school very confused and upset. When she got home from school, she laid across her bed and cried continuously in hopes that her mother would be there and hear her cries for help. But her mother wasn't there to hear her cries. Even though her mother neglected to be there for her due to work, she still loved her very much.

Maryann stayed in the house and away from her friends for a couple days. She felt that it was her fault what her brother had done to her. All this pain she was holding in because she was afraid to tell her mother and father what had happened to her. As time passed on her brother was still molesting and raping her but she didn't dare tell anyone out of fear for her life.

Maryann started liking boys and would always hang around boys and did all the things the boys were doing; she became a tomboy. On the days she wasn't acting like a tomboy, she would dress up and wear her mother's lipstick without her knowing. Every day after school, she would stop by one of her friend's house for her to do her eyes; she would have her show her how to use eyeliner but her mother never knew until one day she came home with her eyebrows plucked.

Her mother asked her if she had plucked her eyebrows and she said no; her mother yelled and yelled at her and told her that she was a little girl and was too young to be wearing make-up. Maryann repeatedly kept insisting that there was nothing wrong with her eyes and that she wasn't wearing make-up. Her mother kept trying to get her to see that make-up was only for adults.

But Maryann didn't think that she was too young for make-up because she was growing up fast and all the other girls were wearing it. She then started hanging around the fast little girls and was doing all that they were doing. She thought she was grown wearing make-up, dressing in skimpy clothes, stuffing her bra with tissue and kissing boys. She had no idea that all this was stemming from what her brother had done to her. In her mind she was acting as a normal child that was just growing up.

During this trying time in her life she was faced with illusions and distractions that would interfere with her schooling and everyday life. She would dream and have thoughts of what her brother had done to her but she still hadn't informed her mother. She carried on as normal and tried not think about her situation because she was still afraid to tell her mother and father. She always asked herself why her brother had done that to her and why she had to be the one that had to go through something like that. The presence of her brother was always a creepy feeling that she had; she hated him for what he had done to her. She felt her brother didn't love her because of what he had been doing to her. She would constantly try to distance herself from him but that was hard to do because they were brother and sister that lived in the same house. But whenever he entered a room that she was in, she would remove herself from that area because she was uncomfortable around him. No-one ever knew or noticed that she was distancing herself from their brother or that she was afraid of him. They just thought that she was being a naughty little girl that always caused trouble in the house. In all reality she felt violated and trapped in a bad situation with not one person to turn to.

In the meantime, her cousin Jonathan started spending the night on the weekends and it was fun to have him over until one night while she was asleep, he came into her room and started fondling her; she woke up and fought him off. The next morning she went and told her mother but her mother didn't believe her for reasons unknown and every time her cousin would spend the night he would fondle her and her sister but her mother never believed their accusations and still continued to allow him to spend the night and Maryann would be so afraid because now it was her brother and her cousin doing these things to her. Maryann was feeling very awkward and so alone that she turned to alcohol to ease her pain; she even started going out with boys and started having problems in school and was fighting more and more every day. She became disobedient and a troublesome child that caused problems all the time due to what she was going through. Inside her mind this was wrong for her to be treated in that manner but no-one would believe her, so she kept it to herself; it was her little secret. She and her sister would talk about their cousin coming over and touching them but she never mentioned anything about her brother out of fear; they would say to each other that they didn't understand why their mother still allowed their cousin back in the home when he was doing those things to them. They both were hurt inside and knew that it wasn't normal or right for them to be fondled; they also felt that their mother had let them down.

By the time Maryann turned twelve, she was out of control; she was drinking, staying out late and was doing poorly in school. Her mother got called up to the school several times because of her behavior but never wondered what was going on with her. She was too busy worrying about work instead of her child; she hadn't even noticed her behavior at home because she was too occupied with work and tired once she arrived home. On her off days she never spent time with her children because all she did was sleep. Maryann was doing poorly in school but she still had good grades;

she was on the honor roll. Her problem was fighting, talking back to the teacher and disrupting the class. When it was time for a test, she would disrupt the class by throwing chairs across the room for no reason and hitting people in the back of the head. She was labeled as a smart kid but a trouble maker. When it was time for lunch, she would randomly push someone down the stairs for no reason and the teacher always knew it was her that had done it. She had gotten suspended from school many times for her behavior that her mother still didn't see any kind of sign as to what was going on with her.

Maryann wanted desperately to tell her parents but she just didn't know how to and felt she would be the one to get in trouble for what happened to her. She was a bitter little girl with no one to turn to. In hopes that it all would end she continued her life normally visiting her friends and staying away from home; returning only when it was time for her curfew. She and her friends would play the piano and enjoy each other time together; they felt like sisters and she felt safe at her friend house. She started spending the weekends with her friend and they would always have fun because no one was messing with her. She never wanted to go home but she knew she had to whenever Sunday came and it would be a hard thing for her to do. Maryann tried to be a normal little girl whenever she was with her friend and she was being a pleasant little girl because she was never in trouble; it was always a pleasure for her friend family to welcome her in their home. Her friend mother would get up and make breakfast for them and treat her like she was her own child. Maryann loved her friend mother and wished that her own mother could be like that, she also wished that she was her own mother. She felt like she was included in their family because of the way she was being treated while she was there.

The days that Maryann was on her block, she would go a couple of houses down from hers to visit another friend and at times her older sister boyfriend Carlos would confront her in the hallway; he would pull her to the back of the hallway and be kissing and fondling her. She would fight him off and run away frantic and afraid to visit her friend. She would then start meeting her friend outside and when she saw her sister boyfriend she would just cringe from the thought of what he had been doing to her. Maryann was having a rough time dealing with her life that she started getting serious about this one boy that she was messing around with. She would constantly sneak over to his house to see him because she liked him a great deal and she felt safe with him because he never violated her in any way. He treated her with respect and cared for her a lot; they were very close. Maryann and her new boyfriend Joe would always have a good time together; they talked about a lot of things but she never informed him of what had been happening to her but Joe knew that something was going on with her but he didn't know what it was. He knew she was going through something because she only really went around him when she was feeling down.

As time passed on, Maryann was still seeing Joe and they fell in love and was very happy that they started talking about marriage and someday having children when they got older. Maryann was still dealing with emotions of being sexually abused by three people and often would try to tell her parents but they never had time to sit down and talk privately with her because her brothers and sisters was always around. She and her sisters were very close but she never told them what was going on with her. All she knew was what her brother had threatened to her and that's all she thought about. She would cry all the time and leave the home and come back late at night. She always panicked whenever she was left alone with her brother but he never touched her again.

When she turned fourteen, Maryann was in a state of mind whereas she felt unloved and would always try to confront her fears through drinking and acting out. But this was not helping her situation at all. She always tried to stay away from her house because of what she was going through; she would always be at her friend house around the corner and never wanted to go home but she had to because she had nowhere else to stay. Maryann had thought constantly about suicide because she didn't know how to deal with what was going on with her, she kept everything bottled up inside of her until one day she snapped.

She went to pay Joe a visit and had planned on telling him what she was dealing with. Once she arrived to Joe's house he was with his family and friends and didn't have time to sit down privately and talk to her because they were having a party. She begged and pleaded with him to listen to what she had to say but he kept insisting later that they would talk. Maryann left Joe's house full of tears and was on a mission to confront the people that had molested her. While walking towards her home she stopped by the store and bought a pocket knife and as she walked, she kept thinking about what she was going to do to the people that had hurt her. The first person she was going to see was her brother and tell him how much of a terrible brother he was to her. As she got close to her building, her brother wouldn't be the first person she would encounter; it would be her sister's boyfriend Arthur. He was standing outside of her building waiting for some friends. Maryann spotted him and walked faster and faster to her building and rushed over to him with the pocket knife in her hand; she stood on her tippy toes and leaned towards him and had the knife to his chin and whispered to him; if he'd ever touched her again she would kill him in a heartbeat. He pushed her away and yelled so do it then little girl; Maryann pulled her hand back and lunged to stab him in the chest but she missed and ran away frantic to a neighbor's house. Her neighbor asked her if everything was ok with her but she insisted that she was fine. She kept peeking out of the window to see if he had left her building so that she could go home. Once she noticed he was gone, she went to her house and was confronted by her older sister; her sister started yelling at her and asking her why she had tried to stab her boyfriend and all Maryann could do was cry. Her sister slapped her and told her that she was going to tell their mother when she got home from work.

Maryann left the house and went three blocks away to her best friend house. She told her best friend what she had just done and that she was going to runaway out of fear for her life. She asked her friend if she could make a phone call before she left. She called Joe and told him what she had just done and how she was not going back home. Joe asked her where she was because he wanted to talk to her in person; she told him where she was and he came within thirty minutes. When Joe arrived there he was anxious to see Maryann and consoled her; he hugged her and asked her if she was alright but she said that she wasn't. Maryann and Joe went for a walk, they then walked to his house but she still didn't tell him what was going on with her or why she had just tried to stab Arthur. She kept telling Joe that she didn't want to talk about it, that she just wanted him to hold her and never let her go. As he was hugging her, she lifted her head up and started kissing him. They started indulging into sexual activities because of Maryann wanting to have sex with him.

I don't think this is what she really would have done if she wasn't dealing with issues and emotions that were driving her crazy. She was confused, distraught, afraid and really not herself. Joe convinced Maryann to go back home and inform her mother of what she's been dealing with because he couldn't help her if she won't tell him. She went back home that night but got into an argument with her brothers and sisters because she was gone all day. The next morning when she seen her mother, she asked if she could talk to her because she has a problem.

Her mother said yes, you do have a problem and you need to get your act together and straighten up or you're going to be in big trouble.

Her mother never let her get to say what she wanted because she was too busy yelling at her and telling her how she was causing trouble at home and in school. Maryann felt that everyone was against her and that she had no one she could trust or love her besides Joe.

She eventually ran away and no one knew where she was; she was a confused little girl with no one to help her. She would walk the streets all alone late at night; she had nowhere to go, no money and no food. She was sleeping on the streets trying to find a way to help herself get out of her situation. A week passed and she thought of calling one of her cousins in order to stay over at their house. She called her cousin Barbara but she was upset with her because she left home and had her parents worried about her; she informed her cousin that things were not right at home. Her aunt ended up going to pick her up and took her back to their house and got her cleaned up and asked her what was going on with her. She just told her aunt that she felt no one loved her because she's always in trouble. Her aunt called her parents and told them that she found Maryann and that she was safe with her.

Maryann's parents rushed to her aunt house and yelled at her non-stop because they were worried about her and thought that something had happened to her. Maryann just looked at them in despair and just cried and cried but still never told them what she was dealing with. When it was time to leave,

Maryann said that she didn't want to go home just yet.

Maryann's aunt intervened and told her parents that she could stay with them for a little while and she would try to figure out what was going on with her; the parents agreed and left but never gave Maryann a hug or kiss.

Maryann's parents didn't know what was wrong with her, they just thought that she was looking for attention by acting out and doing things out of the ordinary. They never considered that someone was messing with her or that she's been molested. All they seen was that her behavior was changing. Her mother wasn't really trying to figure out what her problem was because she never asked her or would always say that she didn't have time to talk and the two times that Maryann did try to talk to her, she didn't believe her and told her that she needed to straighten up. Her father was also busy and had stopped getting them on the weekends, so he had no clue of how Maryann was acting because she or her mother never told him about her behavior.

When Maryann's parents left, she felt worse than she did. She told her aunt that she knew that her parents didn't love her because they didn't even give her a kiss or a hug.

Her aunt informed her that it wasn't true and that they were just upset.

Maryann said, yes auntie I understand but they haven't seen me in a week and they didn't even show me how worried they really were besides yelling at me.

Auntie how can they love me and they just ignore my feelings?

Her aunt said, Maryann, they love you but how would they know what's going on with you if you don't tell them?

Maryann, just said to her aunt that she understands and walked away and went in the room with her cousin. She talked to her cousin about her boyfriend Joe but never told her cousin what's been happening to her. She and her cousin were very close and always did things together because they didn't live far away from one another. She had called Joe and told him where she was and that she needed some time for herself to get herself together; he agreed and told her to call him whenever she was well. He cared for her a lot and wanted nothing but the best for her; he always tried to convince her to tell her parents that something was going on with her, but she never wanted to.

The time came for Maryann to go home and face her fears but she still didn't dare to tell anyone her secret. She tried to focus on being a good sister and student at school but she was still facing these thoughts that were running throughout her mind. Inside her mind she was wanting to just blurt it out but she was afraid to. She just held it in and continued on like if nothing ever happened to her. She then started doing well in school and at home; she was on the honor roll and became a role model to her family. Her mother was very proud of her for being a good child after all. It was very hard for Maryann to just put it all behind her because she had to see these same people every day that had done wrong to her but she somehow managed to move on. She started investing her time in reading and going to the Library.

She didn't mind walking to the Library which was ten blocks away because it helped clear her mind. She would just walk the blocks hopping and skipping enjoying her time alone. Once in the library she would gather up books to sit down and read; she read a lot of books on abuse but none caught her eye. She walked to a librarian and told her she was doing a project at school and was looking for books about inappropriate touching. The librarian pointed her in the direction for the books to gather up. As she got to the section, she saw so many books that she didn't know which one to choose; she grabbed three off the shelf and checked them out.

As she walked home, she was flipping through the pages and one caught her eye.

She said to herself, this is the one I am going to read first.

She walked home hoping that by reading these books it would help solve her problem and give her answers as to opening up to her mother. She read all three books but still felt uncomfortable and didn't get anywhere with the books because they were too mature for her to understand. A week went by and she still couldn't find answers from what she had been reading. She returned the books and felt the same way she did previously.

Months went by and she was still having trouble coping with her situation, she tried to be strong but she wasn't strong enough because she had low self-esteem and still was having suicidal thoughts; she still was drinking and her hormones was getting the best of her. She didn't know how to deal with it and ended up acting out again; she started fighting again at home and in school. Maryann was not the type of girl that told people her problems; she always kept things bottled up inside of her. In the back of her mind, she always felt it was her fault. She would constantly think about cutting her wrist or swallowing a whole bottle of pills; she even thought about running in front of a car. All she wanted to do was end her life because she felt unloved but she never had the courage to kill herself. She wanted nothing but her mother and father to be together and be there for her in order for her problems to go away. She knew her life was not supposed to be the way that it was because none of her siblings was acting like her; they were different and never gotten into trouble or felt the way that she did.

Maryann, wanted so bad to tell someone what she'd been dealing with but she never told anyone because she thought no one would believe her. Now she had to keep dealing with this all alone; she felt as if her family had let her down especially her mother and brother. Maryann was a confused little girl that felt helpless in a cold world. She felt angry and betrayed all the time and needed both her parents. She thought that if her parents got back together then her life would be much better and she would be a normal kid like the others. She tried to convince her parents to get back together numerous times but they didn't; she would hear her mother and father arguing on the phone and hear her mother crying. Maryann would be feeling sorry for her mother and put her feelings to the side; she would console her mother and tell her that everything was going to work out and get better for her. She ended up spending more time with her mother when she wasn't working; they would listen to music and read together. She and her mother became very close and her mother would talk to her about her and her father's problems; Maryann became her confidant. They started bonding more and Maryann had forgotten about her own problems because she was focusing on making sure that her mother was doing well. She would go visit her mother sometimes at work when she got out of school. They were getting along very well and Maryann was still hoping that her parents would make up and get back together.

Maryann started doing other things after school to ensure that her pain and anger didn't come back and get the best of her again. She signed up for dance classes and was doing very good until one day she had a breakdown because her mother failed to show up to see her perform. Her mother had missed four of her performances and this one was important to Maryann. Maryann felt betrayed once again; she felt as if her mother had let her down like she's done in the past. She started getting migraine headaches and she would cry practically all day and night because the pills she was taking was not helping her headaches. Her mother took her to the doctors several times but they didn't know what was causing her headaches. She fell into a depression and started having scary dreams and thoughts again of what had happened to her. Now she really wanted to harm herself because the thoughts were back and she was miserable. She was in an uneasy state of mind because every time she had gotten it off her mind, something would trigger it back and this was not helping her at all. Maryann had plenty of cries for help but they were always ignored by her mother. She often wondered if her mother loved her and why she couldn't see her pain.

She started looking for comfort in order to ease her pain; in return she turned to Joe again and they would be together all the time. Joe had helped her get herself together and clear her mind.

She then started hanging out with her old friends and would be doing bad things in the neighborhood.

She was stealing out of grocery stores, department stores and drinking. Maryann felt as if she was mature enough to think on her own and make wise decisions. But she was making bad choices because of her actions. Maryann was losing her mind and thought that if she got back at the people that had hurt her, she would get better. Joe stayed with her through all that she was dealing with and had finally helped her to get well and they fell in love. She loved Joe and felt he was the only person she could ever trust because he was always there for her. She focused her time and energy on school and Joe that she was doing much better than ever before and she was a happy person that had gotten over many fears in her life.

As the years went by she had blocked out the bad memories of what had happened to her as a child. She and Joe got married and had twin boys; she tried to be a good mother to her children but it was hard because the babies crying would be making her nervous; this was something she was not used to. She eventually learned how to care for her children and she loved them more than anything in the world. She spent all her time devoted to her husband and sons that she stayed focus on them until one day while her husband was at work and she was at home caring for the twins, she sat on her bed to watch television, she seen that a talk show was coming on. Maryann sat there watching the talk show and the topic was about molestation; she started shaking, trembling, panicking and visioning all that had happened to her in her younger life. She cried and cried profusely in hopes that it was a dream. She turned off the television and called her mother weeping on the phone, her sister answered and asked, Maryann is that you? She sobbed more, said yes and asked to speak with her mother. Her sister asked her if everything was alright and told her that their mother was at work. Her sister tried to fill her with words of comfort to figure out what was wrong with her.

She replied, "I've been raped and molested practically all my life!!"

Her sister replied Maryann, what are saying? Are you sure?

Maryann cried more and asked her sister to come over to be with her. Her sister rushed over to her house only to find Maryann sitting on the floor in a deranged state of mind holding a knife, jabbing it into the floor over and over and blurting out the words "I'm going to get revenge on the people that hurt me, this is not the end!" Her sister tried repeatedly to get her up off the floor but Maryann wouldn't budge; she finally held Maryann in her arms and told her how much she loved her but Maryann still wouldn't snap out of it because her mindset at that time was still unstable. Her sister frantically called her mother to inform her of Maryann's mental breakdown; her mother rushed to her daughter's house and held Maryann and sat her on the couch.

She said, "Baby I'm here, please tell mother what's wrong with you."

But Maryann kept crying and crying and finally informed her mother of what had happened to her in the past. Her mother held her more and told her that everything was going to be alright and that they would try to fix the situation.

She asked Maryann why she hadn't told her this when it had been happening. Maryann said I tried to tell you many times but you were too busy; she stayed with Maryann a little while longer and helped her pull herself together. Maryann told her mother that it was her fault and that she should have always put her first instead of work; she blamed her mother over and over and made her mother upset. Her mother left crying but told her that she loved her.

Later that night when her husband arrived home from work, she told him she had a confession to make to him about what she's been dealing with over the years. They sat down and had a talk; In the meantime, she informed him of everything that had happened to her and he was very upset but supportive towards her and told her that he would set her up for counseling sessions so that she could get herself well and be able to move on with her life now that she has opened up and let the information out.

However, as the days passed, Maryann's mother never even told her father what was going on or confronted the people that had hurt her daughter and never called the police to get involved. Maybe she didn't believe Maryann or felt it was a long time ago and it didn't matter. Her mother never called her as the days went by to check on her to see if she was alright. Her mother had let her down again and she felt that she should have never told her mother because her mother was never there for her whenever she needed her as a child and it was even more clearer to her that she was right as a child when she thought her mother wouldn't believe her. Maryann felt animosity towards her mother and said she would never speak to her again for allowing that to happen to her. She felt that if her mother was home more often that it would never have happened to her. She felt as though she was just all alone in a cold world.

As time passed on, Maryann ended up falling into a deep depression again and it would interfere with her marriage due to her having the bad images and nightmares again. She constantly would wake up in a rage and wouldn't allow her husband to touch her; she would constantly fight her husband Joe because she would be having visions of her brother, her sister's ex-boyfriend and her cousin touching her at that moment. Her husband would always try to convince her to go back to counseling because she only went a few times and refused to go back; she felt it wasn't helping her and for her to have to recollect those memories was too painful. Maryann ended up telling her husband that she needed to go away for a while to clear hear mind; she left and went to stay with her cousin Barbara.

Maryann stayed with her cousin Barbara for three weeks and was doing a little better, she tried to focus on herself and get her thoughts under control but she still was confused and turned to alcohol again. She started drinking, sleeping around with guys she didn't know, going out to parties and sometimes wouldn't return to her cousin house. She was out of control and she was proving this everyday by her actions; she stopped calling her husband and her sons and started hanging around with the wrong crowd of people and she became a person on the verge for vengeance. She called her cousin one day and told her that she was going to kill the people that destroyed her life. Her cousin tried to talk her out of it and told her to let the police know what happened to her but she refused to call the police. Maryann thought that her cousin was against her and hung up on her; she felt that this was something she had to do so that they wouldn't hurt anyone else.

However, she walked around the neighborhood looking for someone she could buy a gun from; she had a plan in motion and thought that this would solve her problem; she never even considered the thought of her getting caught. She just knew that she had a plan and she was going to get it done once and for all. Maryann found someone to buy a gun from and proceeded on with the idea to kill the ones that had hurt her in the past. Although, she thought about how and when she was going to do it. She knew getting them all together wouldn't be a hard thing to do because they all hung out together; she thought of getting them one by one but thought it would be too hard to do; she was contemplating on not one murder but three and felt she would get away with it. Maryann was out of her mind and felt no-one knew what she was going through and felt the pain that she was enduring. She always felt alone and thought her mother didn't love her enough because she didn't see that she was being molested as a child.

Maryann was devastated and still seeking out revenge on the three that had hurt her; she was trying to find the right time to commit murder. She had thought this out carefully and knew that it would work for her. She didn't care that one of them was her brother and the other was her cousin; all she thought of was how much they had hurt her and wasn't going to get away with it because she was going to make them pay for what they had done to her.

In the meantime, she let time pass by because she had told her cousin Barbara what she was going to do and didn't know if her cousin had told anyone; she was trying to buy some time so that she wouldn't get blamed for it. She tried to act normal and pretend like nothing was bothering her and that she had put the thought out of her mind. Eventually she went back home to see her husband and children, she told her husband that she was well and that she wanted to move on with her life and be a happy family again. She told her husband how much she loved him and how sorry she was for leaving. But her husband didn't believe her; he told her that he talked to her cousin and found out that she'd been partying, drinking and became infatuated with the idea to commit murder.

She looked in shock and said, why no! I've been doing just fine and I have been getting myself together; she's just mad because I've found new friends.

Nevertheless, Joe still didn't believe Maryann and told her she needed to get herself together or he wanted a divorce because she was ruining his and the children lives. But Maryann refused to accept that; she kept implying that she was fine and reassured him that she would never leave them again. Her husband informed her that he would give her one more chance to get her act together or they would be through for good. They worked it out and Maryann had to now move on or confront her fears on her own.

While Maryann worked on being a wife and mother, she still found herself unable to get the thoughts out of her mind. She tried everything that she could but nothing worked for her. Basically, she now was dealing with facing her fears or losing her family and she had a major choice to make. She knew her husband would be there for her and help her through this horrific ordeal but she just wanted revenge. She would now take the time to think of several options she could pick to get herself well. Her constant thoughts were: she could go to counseling sessions, she could confront her brother and cousin and get some answers from them, she could go to the police, or just forget about it. She was trying to consider ways of getting to the bottom of everything in order for her to move on with her life. She was finally really thinking this through because she didn't want to lose her family.

Although Maryann had these tough decisions to think about, she needed to do this immediately in order for her to be happy and have progress with her family because her family needed her. She also needed to get herself together because she was falling apart. This was something she had carried around for a very long time and didn't allow her to be a normal child. Her mind was so messed up and confused with the thoughts of what had happened to her that she didn't know how to confront it or get over it. She had dwelled on it for so long that it stuck in her mind and once she finally had let it go, it came back to her mind while watching television. Maryann had let the thought of molestation dictate her life for so long that she blamed herself and her mother. She started feeling that it wasn't just molestation; it was incest by her family members and they needed to be responsible for how she turned out and get punished for it. She kept thinking of ways to move on with her life and put it all behind her because she didn't want to lose her family or lose her mind by going crazy. She always wondered why this had happened to her by her family members and this was a thought that always stuck in her head. In her mind, she felt this had to be happening somewhere down the line to others in the family but no one ever said anything about it; she felt it was a family secret that went on for a very long time and had to be hereditary, but now she would be the brave one to confront it because it had destroyed her life. She constantly thought of how she was a mean little girl towards her friends, had messed up in school and was fighting all the time and this was the reason why. Her mind was always filled with hatred and she expressed it with violence and alcohol daily when she was growing up.

As the days would pass her by, Maryann would be reflecting back on the life that she had as a child and growing up; she discovered that she grew up faster than the others. She engaged in sex before anyone else and was living as if she was a grown up. She was always confused and devastated of the thought. She ended up getting depressed again and on a day that she was under presser, she took her gun out of a shoe box and decided to learn how to use it. With this thought on her mind, she felt as if it would ease her pain and leave her with an easy state of mind. Now that she had a gun, she felt in control and figured that no-one would mess with her; she would be in control from here on out. She didn't even know how to use a gun but would try to learn how to use it on her own. She often went to open grassy fields and set up bottles and would shoot at them. The bottles were her target practice and she definitely was learning how to shoot because she was getting better and better with practice. This also was relieving tension off of her; she was doing much better but would start to think that having a gun wasn't a good idea. She was tired of sneaking out and hiding the gun from her husband that she threw it in the river. The thought of her husband finding out that she had a gun and had been practicing how to use it would be devastating to him and he would know that murder was still on her mind and he would leave her for good. Maryann didn't want to lose her family because she loved them too much.

She now had another plan in motion and felt that it would help her with some kind of closure. She wanted to call her brother and cousin and speak to them directly about sexually molesting her in order for her to get it off her chest. She thought this would be a good idea and wanted to handle it on her own.

Maryann talked to her husband about her plan and he agreed to it; she and her husband picked a day that they would make the call. She initially called her brother and set up the meeting and when that day came for the arranged meeting with him; she was afraid to meet with him alone so her husband sat in with her. Once her brother arrived he acted like a normal brother because he didn't know what the meeting was about; he didn't know that she had told her husband or that she remembered what had happened. Her husband welcomed her brother into their house and told him to have a seat. He sat on the couch and asked where Maryann was. Maryann walked out of the room and sat in a chair close to her kitchen just staring at him in a rage. Her husband walked over to her and asked if she was alright and had wanted to call it off.

She said no I can do this; she took a deep breath and interrogated her brother.

He tried to act like he didn't know what she was talking about. She told him that she never forgot and always remembered what he had done to her but he still kept denying what he had done.

Maryann stood up and walked over to him and said don't you remember "tell or I will kill you!!" Her brother looked in despair and said, I don't know what you're talking about and still denied it.

She asked her husband if he could step out of the living room for a second.

When her husband left the room, she sat back down and said okay it's just me and you, now talk.

Her brother said, Maryann I was young and I'm sorry,

I didn't know what I was doing.

She said, you did know what you were doing because you were old enough to know right from wrong and I'm your sister.

He kept apologizing and she told him that she would never forgive him because he stole her virginity and scarred her for life. She started to cry but instead she told him to leave her house and never speak to her again.

He said, I'm sorry Maryann, I'm sorry, I was a kid doing kiddy things; she yelled, get out now or else!

Her husband ran out of the room and her brother was still standing there; he pushed her brother out the door and told him to stay away from his wife. Her brother got in his car frantic wondering if she was going to call the police or tell anyone else what he had done. He was afraid that if his parents, wife and friends knew what he had done, his life would be ruined.

Meanwhile Maryann's husband was consoling her while she was crying, he lifted her up and told her that it was over and that everything would be alright and as he was holding her, a shot was fired. They both dropped to the floor and was looking around. They stayed on the floor for a few minutes; once off the floor, they looked outside only to find her brother laying on the ground. Maryann and Joe rushed outside to her brother's aide but it was too late; he had shot himself in the head. They called 911 and when the police arrived, he was pronounced dead at the scene. At that moment, Maryann felt relieved but yet sorry for her brother.

Her husband called the family to inform them of Talbert's death. They all rushed over and tried to figure out what had happened and why their brother would kill himself at Maryann's house. Her husband sent them home and told them that they would talk about it in the morning because Maryann was in shock and talking to the police. When everyone including the police left, Maryann was unstable. Joe held her all night rocking her back and forth until she fell asleep. Maryann woke up the next morning telling her husband she had a bad dream that her brother killed himself.

He told her that it wasn't a dream and that it did happen. Him and Maryann sat on the bed and talked about what happened. She started blaming herself and said that if he had never went to their house that would never have happened.

She said, I didn't want him to kill himself; I just wanted him to know I knew and how it made me turn out.

Joe told her he knew how she felt but it wasn't her fault.

She said, Joe I have something to tell you.

She said, I brought a gun.

He yelled what! You brought a gun!

She said, yes but I threw it away. I was going to kill him myself but I threw it away instead because I didn't want to lose you or the kids.

Joe hugged Maryann and told her that she now has closure and maybe she can move on with her life.

She said that she would try.

Later that day the family came over to talk about what happened; she informed them of what had transpired the night before, triggering Talbert's death. The family was upset and her mother blamed her again.

Maryann said, well why didn't you mention it to him when I told you?

Her mother said, because I didn't believe you and besides, it was a very long time ago.

Maryann said, just as I thought, I knew you never believed me but now you see it was the truth or he wouldn't have killed himself.

Her mother tried to hug her but Maryann shrugged and walked away. Her sisters and her other brother were crying but Maryann wasn't; she stayed calm, cool and collective. She was brave now and told everyone that it wasn't in her intentions for that to happen because she didn't know Talbert owned a gun. She told her siblings how much she loved them and that she was fine with what had happened. Her mother and her siblings then left with the answers they came for.

When the time came for her brother's funeral, Maryann refused to go. She told her husband she wasn't going and didn't care that he was dead because he couldn't hurt her or anyone else ever again. Her phone was ringing constantly on that day but she wouldn't answer, she ended up unplugging her phone. She felt that she now had a little peace within her and didn't have to worry about her brother or what he done to her. She was feeling happy that he took his own life instead of her having to do it and get herself in trouble.

She had no love and showed no pain for her brother's death; it didn't bother her at all that he was gone; in her mind that was the best thing that could have happened. After the funeral, her father showed up at her door wondering why she never made it there. She welcomed her father in her home and informed him of everything that happened to her; he was devastated. He hugged Maryann and told her how sorry he was for that happening to her. He then asked her why she never told him before when she always knew she was daddy's little girl. She informed him that she was afraid to and that her brother had threatened her. He told her that he would always be there for her, if she ever needed someone to talk to. Her father sat with her and Joe for a little while and ate dinner together. He told Joe how thankful he was to have him as a son-inlaw and someone to take care of his daughter. They sat over dinner talking, trying to find solutions for Maryann to get her life on track and as time was winding down it was time for her father to leave. He left and told her that he would call and visit her more often to make sure that she was headed towards recovery.

Maryann said, okay daddy and kissed her father good-bye.

As the days and months passed, some of the family was finding out what really had happened and why Talbert had committed suicide. Everyone was calling Maryann telling her how sorry they were for what had happened to her as a child. She told them that she been dealing with it for a very long time and that he wasn't the only one that had molested her. They asked her who the other person was but she never told them. The family was still upset that Maryann had been molested by her brother and her mother never said anything when she found out. They then would go to her mother for answers as to why she never confronted her son with this information. One of her aunts called her mother and started telling her she wanted answers as to why she never said anything to Talbert; her mother told her to mind her business and hung up. Maryann's mother was feeling guilty because she never said anything to Talbert and hadn't been there for Maryann; she felt she let both of her children down. The two of Maryann's aunts went to pay her mother a visit but she wouldn't answer the door. They left and went back the next day and each time that they went, she avoided them. The aunts yelled from the outside of the door, telling Maryann's mother to open up because she would have to face them one day. Maryann's mother finally opened the door and had let them in; they sat down and talked it over but Maryann's mother kept defending Talbert. The aunts grew angrier with their sister and started telling her to get out of denial.

They said, it was Talbert's fault and he shouldn't have never done that to his sister or anyone; Talbert did kill himself but that was out of guilt and shame. He just didn't want anyone to know what he had done.

They told their sister that if she would have said something to Talbert, it may not have went that far and he would still be there. The mother listened and agreed and said,

I guess maybe you're right. She said, I just didn't know how to go to him with that information; I was trying to figure out how to mention it to him and then he probably would have denied it anyway. The aunts then informed her that she needed to be there for her daughter and help her through this ordeal.

The mother said, but she won't speak to me.

The sisters told her to just call her anyway or go by to see her to make things right between them.

She said that she would.

The sisters left to head home but detoured to Maryann's house.

They informed Maryann that they had just spoke with her mother and wanted Maryann to listen to what her mother has to say whenever she calls or visits. Maryann agreed that she would speak to her mother whenever she called or visited her.

Maryann's mother eventually came to see her; she apologized for not being there for her and for what her brother had done to her. She told her that she always loved her regardless of how she became. She told Maryann that she was always her little angel and that's why she always talked to her about her problems with her father. She and her mother started to spend more time together and they got along well. They talked about seeking justice on her cousin and her sister's ex-boyfriend in order for Maryann to have complete closure and feel safe. They agreed to go to the police department and report the incident whenever Maryann was ready to go.

Meanwhile, Maryann's mother wanted revenge on the two that had hurt her daughter; she called Maryann to set up a time and date to be at the police department. When the day came to go to the police department, Maryann's father showed up with a lawyer to give support. They reported the incident but the police were giving them a hard time and told them that since it was a long time ago, they didn't know if it would hold up in court. The lawyer pushed the issue further and said that he wanted it investigated and have the two brought up on charges.

The lawyer said, I don't care what kind of charges they are charged with as long as these two sickos are off the street.

The officer ran the two names in their database; the cousin had no priors but the sister's ex-boyfriend name came up. The officer went to talk with the sergeant in charge; the sergeant came out and asked if they knew where her sister ex-boyfriend lived because someone else had filed a complaint but they couldn't find him because he had moved out of the area. They gave the sergeant his address and filed a complaint. Maryann left the police department feeling confident that justice would be served; she also was happy that she had her family there to give her support.

In the meantime her cousin was feeling a bit uneasy and kept his distance because he felt the word would get out about him; he was now paranoid. He packed his family up and moved to another area due to his fears. He thought that Maryann would tell the family and his wife. He just couldn't chance the thought of his wife leaving him. But it was too late because Maryann and her mother had already reported the incident to the police. As time passed on, he went about his life like nothing ever happened and he was on the run. He found a job as an auto mechanic and was working there for a few months when the police showed up at his job and confronted him. He denied the accusations but the police took him down to the station and interrogated him more. He told them that he didn't harm anyone and that this was all a big mistake and a lie. The police locked him up anyway and telephoned Maryann to tell her that they had her cousin.

Days later, they picked up her sister ex-boyfriend and interrogated him; he denied it and now had two charges facing him. He kept insisting that he wanted a lawyer; they appointed a lawyer to come speak with him at the station but he kept telling the lawyer that it was all a mix up and it wasn't him. The lawyer told him that he would work to clear his name and find the real person responsible. The lawyer asked him why would Maryann state that he molested her and he said he didn't know because maybe she's confused and upset that her brother did that to her and killed himself and just wanted to blame someone else instead.

The lawyer said okay, I will talk with her.

He immediately said NO! Wait!

He told the lawyer that he was young and just wanted to kiss her.

The lawyer said, this was more than a kiss; she's blaming you for touching her on several occasions.

The lawyer didn't believe what he was saying and told him that he's facing time for two charges of molestation.

He put his head down on the table trying to figure out a way to persuade his lawyer to get him off. The lawyer told him that he would try to get him off on bond or see if they would just let him go for now. They denied his request and locked him up.

Maryann got the call that both her perpetrators were behind bars; she was so relieved. She hung up the phone and called her husband at work and informed him of the news. When he arrived from work, they celebrated with a glass of wine. Her family came over to celebrate with them. They spent the evening talking about Maryann having to stand up in court and face them.

Maryann said, face them, I have to get on the stand?

Her husband said, yes because the juror has to hear both sides or they would get off.

Maryann started to get a little nervous; she kept prancing back and forth and insisting that she's not going to court. She felt trapped and afraid; her husband told her that she would do fine and that she would have family there to support her. She thought about it and still said she wasn't going to court. Everyone felt her pain and agreed that she not testify. When everyone left Maryann's home, she sat down with her husband and told him that she just didn't want to relive what they had done to her.

She said, I don't know, not now but I will think about it.

As the days passed, Maryann was starting to feel comfortable with the idea of testifying because this would solve her problem. She started feeling that if she told her story more people would come out that hadn't before. She felt they had done this to other people and would pay for what they did to her. She started being persistent and would constantly call her lawyer to make sure he wasn't slipping on the case. She was ready to face the two that had hurt her but it wasn't coming fast enough. She became very confident and anxious to go to court; she couldn't wait to get it over with.

Ten months passed and it was time for Maryann to go to court. She was a bit shaky at first because she never been in a courtroom and the thought of her having to get on the stand made her feel uncomfortable. Her husband promised her that she had nothing to worry about and she would be okay. Once they arrived to court; she was nervous about going through the metal detectors and emptying her purse; even though she was a bit afraid, she walked through anyway feeling courageous. After they all went through the metal detectors, they proceeded to the courtroom. Once inside the courtroom she kept looking around at everything in the courtroom; she started to get nervous and ran out of the courtroom. Her husband followed behind her and told her to pull herself together.

He said, Maryann you can do this!

Take a deep breath and focus on putting these predators behind bars!

Don't you remember they hurt you and God only knows who else!

Maryann, took a deep breath and went back into the courtroom. She nervously sat patient in her seat next to her lawyer until it was her turn to testify against them. When it was her turn to testify, she went up and told all that had happened to her; she stopped and cried a little bit and asked for a glass of water. She took a sip of her water and a deep breath and continued on. Once she finished, she walked off the stand feeling as if justice would be served. The court took an hour recess and Maryann talked to her lawyer about the case and how confident she felt. She wasn't afraid anymore and couldn't wait for the hour to be up. When the hour was up, the verdict was in. The judge ordered her cousin five years' probation, one year community service and to be listed as a pedophile because it was so long ago. Her sister's exboyfriend received seven years in jail for two counts of molestation and to be listed as a pedophile.

Maryann stood up and felt a bit upset because her cousin had gotten off but she was satisfied with the outcome being that he did get probation and had to do community service. As she and her family was leaving the courtroom, her cousin called out for her; he went over to where they were and apologized to Maryann and told her that he was deeply sorry for what he had done to her. He told her how sorry he was for putting her through all that turmoil throughout the years. She accepted his apology and told him that she just wanted to move on with her life. She and her family left and went home; they celebrated the verdict and Maryann felt free from her pain and anger.

In her mind, this was some form of closure for her and she now could finally move on with her life and enjoy her family. It didn't matter to her if it was years later that justice was served because she was just glad that it was out and she was free from holding in all that rage and was able to release herself from it. She wasn't that afraid little girl anymore; she discovered how tough she was throughout the years. But for Maryann to have held her secret in for so long it could have nearly destroyed her, but it didn't because she was determined to seek justice. She had faced her fears and was able to move on with her life.

A year later Maryann and her husband moved to New Jersey, brought a new house and had another baby. She protected her family with everything making sure that no-one was going to hurt her babies; she guarded them and took them everywhere she went. She had completed her journey into getting her assailants caught and that was more than she could ask for. Although, her cousin was free, she still was able to move on. Things started to prosper for Maryann because she wasn't having issues with her fears or having horrible dreams. She was in control of her life and became a wonderful wife and mother that wasn't ashamed of what had happened to her; she ended up opening a recovery center for people that were raped, abused and molested. She kept in contact with her family on a regular basis. She and her mother had a stronger bond than ever before and this was the relationship she had always wanted with her mother. She was able to start a new life and be happy with who she had become. Inside her mind, this part of her life was just beginning and she was able to move on.

Printed in the United States
By Bookmasters